The Goatherd
and the Shepherdess

A Tale From Ancient Greece

Retold by Lenny Hort • Pictures by Lloyd Bloom

Dial Books for Young Readers New York

In memory of Papa

L. H.

Published by Dial Books for Young Readers
A Division of Penguin Books USA Inc.
375 Hudson Street
New York, New York 10014

Text copyright © 1995 by Lenny Hort
Pictures copyright © 1995 by Lloyd Bloom
All rights reserved
Designed by Julie Rauer
Printed in Hong Kong
First Edition
1 3 5 7 9 10 8 6 4 2

Library of Congress Cataloging in Publication Data
Hort, Lenny.
The goatherd and the shepherdess: a tale from Ancient Greece /
retold by Lenny Hort ; pictures by Lloyd Bloom.
p. cm.
Summary: As three friends tend their flocks on a Greek island,
Daphnis and Dorcon vie for the affections of Chloe.
ISBN 0-8037-1352-5 — ISBN 0-8037-1353-3 (lib. bdg.)
[1. Greece — Fiction. 2. Herders — Fiction.]
I. Bloom, Lloyd, ill. II. Title.
PZ7.H7918Go   1995 [E] — dc20 93-18178 CIP AC

The art consists of acrylic paintings,
which were reproduced in full color.

Protect our flocks from wolves.
Protect our children from bandits.

The shepherds on a certain Greek island
used to pray every day to the god Pan,
who was half man and half goat.

EARLY one morning an old shepherd crept into Pan's sacred cave, not to pray, but to shoo out a mother sheep that had strayed inside. The old man found the answer to prayers of his own, for a baby girl who had been abandoned by her poor parents was suckling at the ewe's udder. He brought the pretty foundling home, and he and his wife, who had despaired of ever having a child, named her Chloe and raised her as their daughter.

When she was old enough, Chloe was put in charge of the flock and would take her sheep to graze in the hills alongside the flocks of Daphnis, the goatherd, and Dorcon, the cowherd. Now Daphnis too was an orphan foundling; his foster parents had let a nanny goat suckle him just as Chloe had been fed by the ewe. So it was natural that Daphnis and Chloe became the best of friends.

One spring day two frisky billy goats started butting each other over their favorite nanny. As Daphnis tried to part their horns, he tumbled with one of the goats into a deep pit that had been dug as a wolf trap. The billy goat broke both of its horns in the fall, but luckily Daphnis didn't break anything. Chloe and Dorcon pulled them out of the pit.

Daphnis gave Dorcon the injured goat. He asked his friend to go sacrifice it in thanks for his own survival, but the cowherd lingered for a long while before leading the animal away. As Dorcon gazed at Chloe tending to Daphnis's bruises, he found himself wishing that he was the one she was nursing. And Daphnis would have happily broken both of his legs and sacrificed all of his goats if it had meant one more wound for Chloe to wash, massage, or bandage.

So as the days grew longer and hotter, Daphnis and Dorcon grew as frisky and quarrelsome as a couple of billy goats over their favorite shepherdess. The two young men insisted that Chloe judge which of them could play a better tune on the pipes. They also insisted that she award the prize—a kiss. Dorcon piped his heart out and charmed the sheep and cows and goats. But Daphnis won the prize, and Dorcon saw that he'd have to find some other way to win a kiss from Chloe.

That evening Dorcon disguised himself from head to foot in a wolfskin. He hid in a thicket by the spring where Chloe always watered her sheep. There he waited, thinking about how he would leap out and carry her off when she appeared. He waited a long time. The wolfskin made him itch and his leg was cramped from crouching. Then he heard familiar sheep bells and the shepherdess appeared with her flock.

Two sheepdogs charged into the thicket and pinned Dorcon against a thornbush. The dogs tore the wolfskin, and a good deal of his own skin, right off of Dorcon's back. They might have made a meal of him if Chloe hadn't called them off. Poor howling Dorcon didn't even get the satisfaction of having Chloe nurse his wounds. Daphnis laughed as he pulled the thorns out of him one by one, while Chloe rounded up her sheep that had been scared away by all the barking and howling.

After that, Dorcon wasn't much of a rival for Chloe's affections. All that could keep Daphnis and Chloe apart was the harshest winter that anyone could remember, for when sheep stay in their barns, so do shepherds. Yet even when the snow was deepest, Daphnis made sure to walk his dogs, to ice-fish in the pond, to borrow a jar of honey—anything that might bring him past Chloe's cottage.

In time the ice melted, buds opened, and the land grew fat again. Dorcon and Daphnis were watching their flocks by the seaside one afternoon, when the goats scattered and the two of them were surrounded by a troop of pirates. The herdsmen swung their crooks valiantly, but a sword thrust in the back brought Dorcon to his knees. Daphnis was seized along with some dozen cows and forced aboard the pirates' boat. The bandits rowed away, laughing about the good price that the handsome young man was sure to fetch at the slave market.

Chloe had seen it all.

As Daphnis's cries grew more and more distant, she ran to Dorcon's side. "Slaughtered like an ox," he said, smiling sadly. He handed her the pipes that hung about his neck. "Chloe, two last favors for a man running out of breath. Take the pipes and blow the cattle call. As loud as you can, blow! And Chloe, one kiss to remember your poor friend by." Weeping, she kissed him. "Now blow," he said, and those were his last words. She raised the pipes to her lips and summoned all the wind that she could to sound the call, once, twice, three times.

The music carried over the land, over the hills, and over the water. The cattle bellowed and leapt overboard toward the shrill notes calling them home—capsizing the pirate galley in their wake. Few of the bandits escaped being dragged to the bottom by their weapons, but Daphnis grabbed the horns of two young steers and was safely ferried to shore.

Chloe told him what had happened. She did not mention
Dorcon's kiss. But thinking of the dying man made her thank
the gods all the more that the living one was safe in her arms.

The herdspeople buried their slain companion with great honors, pouring out the best of the milk and wine and fruit and flowers on his grave. It was at the funeral that Daphnis and Chloe swore their love and swore never to be parted again.

They were married at harvest time, with great joy and spilling of milk and wine and fruit and flowers.

Their flocks prospered and multiplied, not only sheep and goats, but boys and girls, all growing up under the adoring eyes of the old couples who had raised the two foundlings. Daphnis and Chloe never sought to learn who their natural parents had been. Whether they had been born rich or poor, slaves or princes, they both knew that they could have had no happier fate than that which had brought them together as children of the pasture, nursed by a sheep and a goat.